When You a Baby

By Linda Hayward

Illustrated by Ruth Sanderson

A GOLDEN BOOK · NEW YORK
Western Publishing Company, Inc., Racine, Wisconsin 53404

Amy was a little girl who could do things.
She could zip the zipper on her new blue jacket.
She could pour the cat food into Mr. Tomkins' dish.
She could climb to the top of the jungle gym.

Amy's father called her "my big helper."

Amy's mother called her "my brave girl."

Sometimes Amy was glad she was brave and helpful and big. And sometimes she was glad she was still a little girl.

One day Amy's aunt and uncle came to visit.
They were going to have a baby.
"You can borrow some of Amy's baby things,"
said Amy's mother.
What baby things? Amy wondered.

Amy's father went outside and opened the garage door. Amy rode her tricycle in the driveway. She was watching.

Out of the garage came a black baby carriage.

"Was that *my* baby carriage?" Amy asked.

"Yes," said her father. "When you were a baby, you rode inside. You were very little then."

"How little was I?" Amy wanted to know as she pedaled past her father.

"Too little to ride a tricycle," he said.

Out of the garage came a pink-and-green playpen.
"Was that *my* playpen?" Amy asked.
"Yes," said her uncle. "When you were a baby, you
sometimes played with your toys in here."
"Was there enough room for all my toys?" asked Amy.

"Yes," said her uncle. "You did not take up much space."

"How little was I?" Amy wanted to know as she showed her uncle how she could go over the side.

"Too little to climb in and out," he said.

Amy picked up Mr. Tomkins and carried him into the house.

What is going on in here? wondered Amy.

Amy's mother was standing on a stepladder.
She reached into the closet.
Out of the closet came a small yellow tub.
"What is that?" Amy wanted to know.
"This is a baby bathtub," said her aunt.
"When you were a baby, you took a bath in here."

Amy put the bathtub on the rug and got inside.

"Now it's a big boat," said Amy. "Look at me! I'm sailing on a big blue lake."

"You can hardly squeeze into that tub now," said Amy's aunt. "But it was just your size when you were a little baby."

"How little was I?" asked Amy as she brought her boat to shore.

"Too little for make-believe," said her aunt.

Out of the closet came a red-and-white box.
Inside the box were clothes—clothes that Amy
thought she had never seen before. Amy pulled
out a small pink bonnet.

"Where did we get all these doll clothes?" asked Amy as she put the bonnet on Mr. Tomkins' head.

"These are not doll clothes," said her mother. "These are the clothes you wore when you were a baby."

"Did I wear this bonnet when I was a baby?"
Amy asked.

"Yes," said her mother.

"But it's so little," said Amy.

"You were little, too," said her mother.

Mr. Tomkins leaped up and ran away.
"How little was I?" asked Amy as she
raced after him.
"Too little to chase Mr. Tomkins,"
said her mother.

Amy's father came into the house.
"Where's Amy?" he asked. "Where's my little girl?"

"Here I am!" cried Amy. "But I'm not so little. I'm too big to ride in a baby carriage, and I'm too big to play in a playpen, and I'm too big to take my bath in a baby bathtub, and I'm too big to wear a baby bonnet."

"But you're not too big to hold," said her father.

"And," said her mother as she gave Amy a little squeeze, "you'll never, *never* be too big to hug."